Naturally Amazing

Written by Sunny Y. Royal-Boyd

Illustrated by Taylor Young

Naturally Amazing

ISBN: 978-0-578-79153-1

Library of Congress Control Number: 2020952219

Naturally Amazing

Written by Sunny Y. Royal-Boyd

Illustrated by Taylor Young

On the ride home from school today, Daddy asked Symoné the same question he has asked since PreK-3, "How was your day?" Expecting the normal, "It was good," little did he know he was in for a surprise response.

Symoné turned sideways in the seat to see Daddy's face. She shared with tons of energy and excitement her experience with the Bailey's on the playground during recess.

The Bailey's were a group of girls that most girls wanted to be a part of but, you had to have straight hair and wear makeup. Yeah, makeup on the playground. Symoné's mother was not having it.

She and her friends were jumping rope when the Bailey's approached with hands on their hips and demanded the jump rope.

The girls ignored the first and second requests for the rope. It did not make the Bailey's very happy. Finally, the head-Bailey-in-charge asked with her hands on her hips and frustration in her voice, "Who do you think you are?"

8

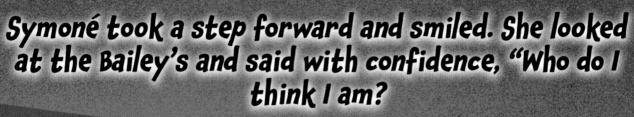

Symoné took a step forward and smiled. She looked at the Bailey's and said with confidence, "Who do I think I am?

I am STRONG like the wind carrying pollen to and from sharing love and life with the earth.

I am **ARTISTIC** like a painter with watercolors creating a portrait to admire today and evermore.

I am INTELLIGENT like Katherine Johnson giving solutions to the wonders of the world from mathematics to politics.

I am GRACEFUL like the movements of a dancer's choreography to the intricate beats of the drum and smooth stroke of a bow on its strings.

13

I am Naturally Amazing; JUST LIKE YOU!

So, when you ask me the question, 'Who do you think you are?' I answer you with affirmation and certainty,

16

I AM *LOVE* and so are you.

Daddy was so proud of Symoné's response. He took her out for a double scoop of her favorite ice cream.

18

He didn't say another word about her day,
but she knew without a doubt she was
LOVED just like YOU!

Dedication

The book is dedicated to my loving Lady Bug as she takes flight and lands during her journey through this life. Land softly and love hard. Cornell, thank you for always encouraging my creativity. Small Guy, thank you for always sharing your view on how I can improve. Mommy, for reminding me, I am the Best Sunny in the world and I am love.

About the Author:

Mrs. Sunny Y. Royal-Boyd is a mother, sister, wife, teacher, and daughter. She and her husband reside in Tampa, Florida with their two children. Sunny is a 20-year educator certified K-12 and found a passion for teaching high school. Sunny enjoys reading, running, and working with children of all ages.

About the Illustrator:

Taylor Young is a freshman at Ringling College of Art of Design in Sarasota, Florida where she majors in Game Art. She has been a member of the Greater Tampa Chapter of Jack and Jill for 11 years. Taylor has been drawing since age 4 and is a member of the National Art Honor Society.

Made in United States
Orlando, FL
01 May 2022

17401409R00015